Candy Kingdom
The Bored Game

Written by
Jenny Griffith

Illustrated by
Elysse Hopkins

For information regarding permissions, write to

Lawley Publishing, Attention: Permissions Department, 70 S Val Vista Drive #A3 #188

Gilbert, AZ 85296. www.LawleyPublishing.com

"This book is dedicated to Catherine, her imagination, and her grumpy cats."

The Candy
Spearmint Hills
Chocolate Fudge River
Chocolate Lake
Licorice Stick Forest

Table of Contents

Bored to Death

Ellie did not want to spend a whole week of summer break with her brother Zeb at their Grandma Gretchen's house. It smelled weird there, and the only kind of cookies Grandma liked to make had raisins in them.

But worst of all, Grandma Gretchen didn't have a television. No *Captain Firestarter*, no *Grunting for Money*, no *Eating Dares*.

"I hate that we will miss the first episode of *Eating Dares*." Ellie leaned her head against the window of the minivan and groaned. "Now we won't know who is going to get stuck tasting the wormy spaghetti."

"Maybe Grandma Gretchen got a computer this year." Zeb laughed without smiling.

"Grandma Gretchen will get a python before she gets a computer," Ellie moaned. Trees blurred past the car. "It's going to be a long, long week."

Back when Grandpa Ronny was around, Grandma's house hadn't been so bad—it was fun, actually. There were games and laughs and candy. However, Ellie could barely remember that time. These days, a lot of rooms were locked up, which didn't help the electronics-free situation.

Zeb rubbed the side of his head. "Gordo McTwigg told me about his uncle who died of boredom."

"Nuh-uh." Ellie had heard Gordo's wild tales before.

"Uh-huh. I asked Dad, and he said it's technically possible."

"To die? Of boredom?"

"Yup. Dad called it the *Fun Ratio*." Zeb was eleven, so he assumed he could use words like ratio without sounding like he was faking intelligence.

"What are you talking about? Fun Ratio?" Oh, brother. Zeb and Dad and their theories.

"You know how time flies when you're having fun? Like, how five minutes goes a lot faster when you're playing Super Submarines than when you're cleaning your room?"

"Duh. Everyone knows that."

"Well, that's the ratio — the more fun, the faster the time." He leaned in closer, glancing at Mom in the front seat of the minivan. Ellie looked, too. Mom wasn't listening. "The opposite is true, too; the less fun, the slower the time."

That made sense. "Seems obvious."

"Maybe, but according to Dad and Gordo McTwigg, it's theoretically possible to have so little fun that time slows and slows until it feels like forever between the ticks of the clock—or the beats of our hearts. Until . . ." Zeb made a croaking sound and drew a line across his neck.

Ellie gasped. "Bored to death."

Zeb's mouth pressed into a grim line as he nodded.

Grandma Gretchen's house was so full of chores and empty of electronics that it looked more likely to be a place to die such a death than anywhere else in the civilized world. A week could turn into . . . eternity!

Mom pulled their minivan into a long, grassy driveway, and Ellie's heart dropped into her stomach. There was Grandma Gretchen, standing on her back steps, waving—and holding a plate full of raisin cookies. Ellie thought she might cry.

"Hello," said Mom, not even getting out of the car. She never got out of the car anymore at Grandma's, but Ellie was sure she used to. "Thanks so much. I'm sure these two weeks will just *fly* by."

Wait. What? *Two* weeks?

BUILD
MAGAZINE

Mr. Grumpy Pants' Bedroom

Grandma Gretchen hugged Mom good-bye through the van window. "Bye, dear. We'll be just ducky here. Hey, kids, that rhymed." With a huge grin, she sent Mom off, and the minivan's tires spewed gravel as Mom sped away. "Come on. I have something new to show you."

New? Nothing new ever happened at Grandma's house.

"Did you get a television?" Zeb asked, his voice dripping with hope. Tonight was this season's first episode of *Eating Dares*. Wormy spaghetti!

Grandma must not have heard him. "Knitting is such a creative process. This new oven mitt design has a cat on it that looks just like Mr. Grumpy Pants."

Oh, dear. Knitting?

Following Grandma with lumbering steps, Ellie dragged her suitcase that was filled with only one week's worth of clothes. Great. Now she was going to have to do laundry. Wash, dry, fold, repeat. But not Zeb. He'd probably just wear dirty clothes, knowing him.

Grandma paused in the kitchen and rummaged in a drawer. It smelled weird in here—like medicine and stale bananas and cat, meaning Mr. Grumpy Pants.

"See? The face? Looks just like him!" Grandma grinned, holding out the potholder pattern. Grandma and her crafts. And they were always weird ones. "I knew you'd like it. And guess what else is new? I've got some exciting canning bottles, too! Look, they have embossed fruit on the side, and they're filled with veggies from the garden."

After Grandma took them to see the bottles of green beans and tomatoes she had canned and placed in the pantry, the excitement was pretty much over.

Ellie looked at Zeb. Zeb was staring up at the ceiling as if he wished heaven would take him now.

"This afternoon, I thought we could weed the garden. By the end of the week, we'll have some ripe vegetables—radishes, oh, and rhubarb. Maybe some rutabagas. You like rutabagas." Grandma winked at Ellie, probably because she'd forgotten that rutabagas made Ellie afraid.

"You know, it's *R week* in the garden. Radishes, rhubarb, and rutabagas, ha-ha-ha-ha!" Grandma had a laugh like a waterfall. It was sweet, unlike her garden vegetables. "And then if you'd like, we can make another batch of raisin cookies. Another *R* food! I pulled these out of the freezer. They're the last of my stash from Christmastime."

Not only were they raisin cookies, these were *old* raisin cookies. And since raisins were old grapes, that made these particular raisins *old*, old grapes. Ellie looked up to heaven too, mostly so she wouldn't have to see the cookies. These were sandwich-type cookies like Oreos—except instead of chocolate cookies, these were sand-colored, and instead of creamy filling, raisin paste was wedged between the discs.

"That sounds great, Grandma. Or maybe we could find a different recipe. Do you like sugar cookies?"

"You know I only eat natural sugars, dear."

"Like raisins?" Zeb asked, munching a cookie.

"Exactly. Fruit sugars are the best. Sometimes I wait until a banana is really ripe and use it for sugar in my recipes. The older they are, the sweeter, you know."

No wonder it smelled like overripe bananas in here. Ellie preferred her sugars un-natural.

Zeb grabbed another cookie and stuffed the whole thing in his mouth. When Ellie coughed, he shrugged at her. "As long as it's food, I'm eating it." He took another one. "Thanks, Grandma."

An hour later, all the raisin cookies were gone, and most of the weeds were out of the radishes. Ellie wiped her brow. Usually, she could avoid summer sun in the middle of the day by watching TV. Grandma moved to another row, the *T foods*, and Ellie followed.

Zeb flipped open his pocket watch. He was eleven and old enough to have Grandpa's old watch. He mumbled while his head bobbed as if he was counting.

"Thirteen days, twenty-two hours and fifty-three minutes," he whispered when Grandma took a bucket of pulled weeds to the trash. "But who's counting?"

Oh, mercy! They'd only been at Grandma's for an hour and seven minutes? It felt like a year already. This could literally be deadly. Ellie pulled a worried grin.

"Is there anything else we could help you with, Grandma?"

R
P

Ellie asked. Zeb shot her a cranky look. "Better busy than bored," she hissed so only he could hear.

Zeb shrugged. "Fine," he hissed back. To Grandma, he said, "We'd love to help. But Ellie looks hot. Got any inside chores or activities we can do?"

Ellie blinked at him. Since when had Zeb ever noticed anything about her comfort?

"Oh, yes, I'm so glad you asked." Grandma sounded happier than she had anytime Ellie had ever heard. "You can help me clean out the back room."

Oooh. The back room that was always locked? Really?

They picked up their garden tools and went in the house—where it was blessedly cooler. Grandma chugged down the hallway, and Ellie followed with Zeb right on her heels.

"I've never seen inside that room. What's in it?" she asked Grandma, trying to sound casual and not like the excited puppy she was on the inside. Puppies were so much better than cats.

"You're old enough now, I think," Grandma said, pulling a key from her housecoat pocket. "Since you're nine, Ellie, and Zeb's eleven, I can trust you in here."

Ellie's tummy did acrobatic flips as the key clicked in the lock. Finally, something new!

Grandma twisted the doorknob. "This, my dears, is Mr. Grumpy Pants's bedroom."

Ellie's tummy's gymnastics clunked to a stop. The cat had its own bedroom?

With a mighty shove that sounded like it toppled something metal behind it, Grandma pushed open the door and flipped on the light. Boxes and plastic storage totes and dust and cobwebs were the theme. And old, yellow paint.

“Don’t step in the litter box,” Grandma said, muscling her way in. “Mr. G. can be territorial.”

If the main part of the house smelled like one cat, this room smelled like a thousand of them. Ellie held her breath. She might have liked Mr. Grumpy Pants if he would quit scratching her whenever they met.

“If we can get this room cleared out enough to get back there, I’ll introduce you to my puzzle closet.” Grandma’s eyes twinkled.

Puzzles! Ellie’s heart jumped back to life.

“I love puzzles!”

Two Mysterious Closets

Not just puzzles, a whole puzzle closet. Well, that sounded promising. Very promising. At least more promising than bottled green beans or anything made of yarn.

Ellie was good at puzzles. Really good. In fact, one weekend, she put a five-hundred-piece puzzle together all by herself.

"Ellie, dear, you'll be glad you're staying with me for two full weeks because I have a *lot* of puzzles."

Ellie looked around the room. A full two weeks might be necessary just to dig their way back to the closet—hey, make that closets. The back wall contained two doors. If one closet was for puzzles, what was in the other?

Oh, right. Probably old yarn.

"You and your puzzles." Zeb groaned from behind Ellie. *Why don't you just enjoy the picture on the box?* he always said. *They look the same, and a glance at the outside of the box takes a lot less time.* "I'd rather watch paint dry than put together a puzzle."

"Shh. Grandma Gretchen will hear you." Grandma was petting

Mr. Grumpy Pants and cooing at him, so she hadn't heard Zeb.

Of course, Zeb was right, but what he missed out on was the joy of the hunt and the thrill of finding a perfect fit. That rush was better than *Eating Dares* and *Grunting for Money* put together.

"Besides, I'm no more obsessed with puzzles than you are with games and trophies, so let's just drop it." She nearly stepped in the large plastic litter box next to the hair-encrusted cushion where the cat obviously slept. Whoa.

She frowned at Mr. Grumpy Pants. Why couldn't her sworn enemy decide to be one of those cats that goes missing for six months? Then he could come back, and the reunion would be so happy for Grandma—and Ellie would be nowhere around. In fact, Ellie wouldn't ask the full six months. Two weeks would do.

Every corner of the dim yellow and brown room was stacked high with boxes labeled with words like "Corn Flakes Sculptures" and "Dried Apple Head Dolls."

"What's a macaroni Kleenex box?" Zeb asked.

Ellie peeked in a box. Corn flakes dyed green had been molded together with melted marshmallow to look like Christmas wreaths or blobs of greenery.

"Grandma Gretchen's crafts sound delicious," Zeb whispered to Ellie. "Except the apple heads." He shuddered.

She didn't disagree. But, how long had the corn flakes sculptures had been sitting there? Why hadn't they attracted mice?

A-ha! Maybe that was why Mr. Grumpy Pants had been assigned to this room.

"Here we are." Grandma had shoved a few plastic totes aside and miraculously made her way to one of the closets at the back. She tugged, and the door creaked like a coffin's lid. Had she forgotten about requiring the kids to clean out the room before getting to see inside the closet? "Puzzles in this closet, games in the other."

"Games?" Zeb said, brightening. "I didn't know you have games. Do you have Super Submarines? I like it because when you win, you get awesome trophies."

Zeb and his trophy obsession. Blah.

"Never heard of that. These were your grandfather's. He loved games." Grandma sounded a little sad. Of course, she missed Grandpa. Ellie could barely remember him, except his white mustache and his happy grin — and the way he always smelled like red licorice.

A low growl sounded behind them, and it grew into a snarl. Out from behind a "Rice and Legume Mosaics" box, Mr. Grumpy Pants launched at Ellie with a yowl. The cat landed his full weight on her chest, his claws digging into her shoulders, his teeth bared.

"Help!" Ellie called. "Vicious cat!"

The cat hissed, and Zeb whirled around, pulling the cat from her chest in a second and tugging it to himself. "There, there, Mr. G. Did mean old Ellie scare you?"

Ellie's jaw dropped. Mr. Grumpy Pants had curled up against Zeb's arms — and he was purring.

"How did you — ?"

"What? I like Mr. Grumpy Pants." He petted the cat, who glared over Zeb's arm at Ellie with a haughty look of triumph.

Ellie pressed her fingers into the scratches on her collarbone and turned back to Grandma, who had started pulling puzzle boxes from the closet.

"Oh, look. Here's one I did a few months ago. It was called 'A Study in Brown.'" Grandma shook the box. "Five thousand pieces.

300
200
5000
3000

Took me all day to put that together."

Ellie glanced at the picture on the box. Three different shades of brown made a swirling pattern, and that was it for the whole puzzle. "Five th-th-thousand pieces, Grandma? And you did it in one day?"

"Well, I couldn't start until after finishing my morning cup of Ovaltine and dead-heading the petunias, so most of a day, I guess." Grandma Gretchen shrugged. "I wish I were faster."

Faster? At a five thousand-piecer? *Whoa.* Had Grandma Gretchen just inadvertently revealed her secret superpower? Because it sounded to Ellie like Grandma Gretchen was a jigsaw puzzle super-genius!

"This one was a little more challenging." Grandma tugged another puzzle from the stack, nodding and smiling at what must have been a pleasant memory. "Ah, yes. 'Winter Scene'."

The picture on the box showed a blank white square. That was the picture for the whole puzzle? Nothing but white? And—this time, the puzzle box said *seven thousand* pieces.

"How long did that take you?" Ellie almost choked as she asked.

"Let me see." Grandma lifted her glasses and read something on the back of the box. "Looks like three days. See?" She held it up so Ellie could read, and there was a start time and a finish time written in marker on the box's cardboard underside. "I guess that makes me a slowpoke."

Ellie looked over at Zeb to see if he was as shocked as she was, but he'd put down the growly cat and disappeared.

Grandma lifted the lid of the snow-only puzzle box and peered inside, her mind clearly elsewhere. Probably on a winter scene far away.

"Zeb?" Where had he gone? Oh, dear. Maybe a pile of crusty craft projects had eaten him. Or worse, he had eaten them. "You still in here?"

"There isn't a single game in here, Grandma." Zeb hollered from the vicinity of the games closet, which was open a crack. A second later, he came out, his arms loaded down with long, flat boxes. "At least no game I ever heard of before."

"Let me see." Ellie stepped over a crate full of glue sticks and silk flowers. "Sorting Socks? Wake the Sleeping Tortoise? Spring Cleaning Chores?" None of those sounded thrilling — at all. "Those games are duds," she whispered.

"Awful," he mouthed back.

Ellie peeked around Zeb to get a better look. Maybe he'd just grabbed the worst ones to be funny. He would do that.

However, as Ellie scanned the titles on the towering stack, none of them looked an *iota* better. See? Ellie could use hard words — when shocked into it.

"Wow, Grandpa really loved games. There are, like, fifty." Ellie inched into the closet, examining the titles. No, make that more than fifty. Maybe a hundred. They were piled two games deep. Some looked like strategy games that could take a whole weekend to play. Strategy games were what Zeb and his friend Gordo McTwigg loved. Except, not these particular subjects. Not "Landscaping Tycoons: Mow, Fertilize, and Weed-Eat Your Way to Wealth."

Zeb set down his first stash of games and, using them as a step stool, reached for something on the top shelf.

"Hey, you're going to smash the cardboard boxes." Broken game box corners turned Ellie into Captain Firestarter — ready to blast flames.

"Who cares? Be serious. Who is ever going to play these games?"

"No one." Ever. But still—broken game box edges! She tugged him off the makeshift step stool. "Just wait a sec. I can bring you a plastic tote to stand on instead." She grabbed a sturdy one labeled "Pasta Art" and slid it at his feet.

"Fine." He leaped up on it and started digging around.

A few boxes fell from the shelves, and Ellie lunged to catch them but failed, and they clattered to the floor. "Watch it, Zeb!"

Zeb didn't watch it. He kept pawing through the pile like a dog after a buried bone. "There's something back there. I can almost—"

An object seemed to glint from the top shelf, piercing through the dim yellow light of the cat's bedroom closet. It dragged Ellie's gaze as if by magnetic force. "Is that . . . gold?"

"It's got raised letters or pictures on it." Zeb stretched up on tiptoe, pushing aside a couple board games to get at it. "I'm not sure. I haven't seen anything 3D in"—he glanced at his pocket watch—"nineteen hours and twenty-six minutes."

But who was counting, right?

"Don't break it." *Please don't break it.* Ellie sucked in a breath as Zeb went on tiptoe again and—with his fingertips—slid the shiny game into the light. Yep, gold! Pinky swear, the box looked like it was covered with real gold.

Something sang in Ellie's ears. Could it be coming from the game?

But as soon as she saw the top of the box, she forgot the singing sound. "Sparklies!" Candy-shaped gems encrusted the top, each a different type of colorful treat. "And Glinties! And Shinies!" Not the tastiest candies, but definitely some of the prettiest. "Open it,

Zeb." Ellie tingled from scalp to toenails. There had to be something amazing, hiding under that golden box lid.

"You're sure?"

"Completely!"

Why would Grandma bury something so beautiful in such a deep, dark corner of a deep, dark closet in a locked room?

"What's going on, children?" Grandma Gretchen shoved aside a stack of boxes and came to check on them.

"Just looking at the games." Zeb could pull off the most casual tone of voice when he tried. "Nothing too exciting."

Ellie couldn't fake a bored face. She bit her lip to keep from letting out another shriek of excitement. The game was singing again and getting louder.

"Oh, no, kids. That one's not a good idea." She lifted Zeb down from his makeshift step stool and pushed it aside. She pressed the game back into its spot and shut the closet.

Click. No more golden, jewel-encrusted game.

It was as if Ellie's cord got unplugged and her system went dark.

"Why not, Grandma?" Zeb whined. These days he only whined when he was truly annoyed. "It looked amazing."

Grandma Gretchen patted him on the head. "You're just like your grandpa. Have I ever told you that? Say, is that his old watch? I'm glad you're getting some use out of it. He loved that watch, told everyone he met that a good watch was the key to everything."

She shuttled them out of the room and relocked the door.

The hallway seemed dimmer than before. The smell of overripe bananas reached its wafting tendrils all the way from the kitchen to tickle Ellie's nose.

She sneezed, and with her sneeze came an idea. Or, maybe it was an excuse.

"But, Grandma," Ellie said in her sweetest voice, "weren't you going to let us do the puzzles?"

Honestly, and to her own surprise, Ellie wasn't nearly as drawn to the puzzles as she was to the golden game box. The singing of the game had fallen silent the moment Grandma clicked shut the game closet door, but for sure, she would be able to hear it again if they could just get back in there. "We can still clear out the bedroom. I'll be glad to help."

"That's generous, dear. Maybe some other time. Today I'm thinking you'd love to learn how to make homemade mayonnaise with me." Grandma herded them toward the kitchen. "Now, you might not know this, but mayonnaise is actually made of emulsified eggs and oil . . ."

Ellie tried to listen to the mayonnaise recipe, but her mind was still floating somewhere beside the door to the closet with the golden game and its candy jewels on top. Somehow, she had to get back there and see inside it. She and Zeb had to think of a way.

The Game is Calling

Two full days — days of pulling weeds, supposedly learning to knit, and dodging Mr. Grumpy Pants's claws — crawled past. The knitting lesson's yarn wadded itself into knots while Ellie's mind was on the closet door.

Zeb had been thinking about it, too. That night, Ellie bumped into him on her way to brush her teeth at bedtime. "What are you doing?"

"Testing something." He twisted the handle on the door to the locked room, but the knob wouldn't budge.

From inside, the cat yowled, and Ellie jumped.

"Should we really be sneaking like this?" Ellie tugged at Zeb's pajama sleeve. "We shouldn't do anything to lose Grandma Gretchen's trust."

"Fine." Zeb gave the lock a last, useless twist. "You saw that game." True, and she'd heard it, too. "It was stuck up on that shelf for a reason."

"Exactly. Because Grandma wants us to stay away from it."

"No, I mean, there's something mysterious, and we need to think of a way to get back in there. I *need* to check out that game."

"I'm not saying you're wrong about the mysteriousness." Ellie was the one who'd heard the singing, after all. "But—" But she had no intention of being dishonest, even for that game.

Finally, she succeeded in yanking him away from the door.

Oh, but that game!

That night, Ellie dreamed about the game.

The next night, Ellie dreamed about the game.

On the fourth day of harvesting rhubarb to boil for lunch and enduring other gardening tasks, Zeb made a mess of Grandma's favorite rosebush while he tried to prune it to her standard.

"Sorry, Grandma. I think it'll survive?" He stated it like a question.

Grandma frowned at the sad little thorny stump, and the stack of rose canes lying on the grass in front of the porch, and muttered something about blue ribbons and the county fair. "Maybe the two of you should do some kind of indoor project."

This could be their opening! Ellie jumped up from her piles of dandelion clippings, brushing off her jacket. "We could clean out the cat's bedroom." Well, that was a sentence she'd never expected to say in her lifetime.

Zeb lit up. "I could help you sort the boxes into a *keep* pile and a *throw-away* pile. Mom said that's how you taught her to stay organized." Zeb gave his movie star smile. Not that Grandma Gretchen noticed, her gaze still on the rose-destruction mess. "It's the best way to keep the clutter down, Mom says."

Grandma pulled her eyes away from the butchered flowers. "Yes, I think that's fine. Here. Take the key. I'm just going to get some rose powder to keep the aphids from . . ."

Zeb practically snatched it from her hand, and both kids took off running.

"We're excited to help, Grandma," Ellie called over her shoulder. Man, they totally looked suspicious. If Grandma Gretchen hadn't been so preoccupied with her ruined flowers, she might have noticed what they were up to.

Down the hallway, Zeb jammed the key in the lock. "Good job picking up on my hint."

"Your hint?"

"You know, when I messed up my outdoorsy job. You said we should come in here."

"Grandma is the one who said we should work inside, not me. But wait. You did that on purpose? Zeb! Those were her best flowers. I heard her say something about a blue ribbon."

"Aw, roses come back. You can whack them right down to the stump." The key twisted, and he pushed the door open. "Hey, kitty." He picked up the cat, which simultaneously purred for Zeb and death-glared at Ellie. "I read all about roses in one of Grandpa's books."

So that's what he'd been doing in the study while Ellie sort of learned to knit. Ellie wouldn't be turning yarn into an oven-mitt-doppelgänger for Mr. Grumpy Pants — or any other creature — anytime soon.

"Still, you should apologize."

Mr. Grumpy Pants wriggled out of Zeb's arms and bolted from the room.

"Fine. Right after we get a look at that game." Zeb shot past the pile of boxes labeled "Frosted Wheat Brick Haystacks" and made a beeline for the games closet. Within two seconds, he'd stacked up a couple of plastic tubs to stand on and had his hands deep into the back of the top shelf where Grandma Gretchen had shoved the game.

"Be careful up there." Ellie kept looking over her shoulder. "Don't—"

"Don't worry. I'm not going to fall."

"I was going to say, 'Don't drop any pieces.'"

"Thanks a lot." Zeb pulled the box from its shelf, and the singing in Ellie's ears began again, louder than ever. "Ta-da!" he said, jumping down from the makeshift ladder. "Flip on the light, and we'll open it."

Ellie vainly waved her hand at the wall behind her, but she couldn't turn on the light because she couldn't peel her eyes away from the game glowing golden in Zeb's hands. It was even prettier than last time. Zeb clutched its bumpy, shiny, delicious glory.

"It's not just Sparklies, Glinties, and Shinies." Ellie's sweet tooth ached, especially after several days of only banana-juice-sweetened oatmeal. "See the flowers decorating the edges?"

"Yeah. They're all candies."

Red jelly hearts, peppermint swirls, chocolate dots. The box's art featured every color of the rainbow. Ellie shivered in sugary enticement. "Ooh! And is that Daffy Taffy?" The candy that told jokes!

"I can't read the title. Come on, Ellie. Switch on the light."

Ellie backed toward the light. Even if Zeb couldn't read the title, she could. "It's *Candy Kingdom*." She said the words, and the singing in her mind went into a high chorus.

Reaching back to where the light switch should be, Ellie's hand landed on something velvety instead.

"A-hem," came the sound of a throat clearing. In a flash, Ellie whirled around and saw that the velvety thing was the shoulder of Grandma's gardening apron.

"Oh, uh. Hi, Grandma Gretchen." Ellie's voice cracked, and shame flooded her. "We were just checking out the one box before we got started, I promise."

Grandma closed her eyes and swallowed visibly. Ellie wished she could sink into the floor. Over by the closet, Zeb's arms trembled, and the game box rattled as it shook.

"I can explain," he said.

Permission?

Ellie and Zeb weren't bad kids. Ellie knew that. Sure, they watched too much TV, and sometimes they'd sneak a flashlight under their covers and read way into the night when Mom and Dad didn't know. But generally, they were obedient, fine kids who just liked to have a good time once in a while.

Normal kids. On the good side of normal, in fact.

And because of that, Ellie's conscience stung. From the look on his face, so did Zeb's.

"Grandma, we're sorry. We know you said not to play that game." Ellie's gaze drifted to the floor. After all Grandma had been doing to entertain and teach them, they repaid her this way? Wrecking her prized flowers and breaking into her forbidden game? A tear sprang to Ellie's eye, stinging it.

Grandma stepped over Mr. Grumpy Pants's litter box and approached Zeb. With slow movements, she took the game from his hands, giving a little laugh.

"Candy Kingdom." She shook the box a little, and from inside came a clinking, as if a hundred tiny pins touched glass prisms. "I'd almost forgotten how vibrant its colors are."

Grandma didn't look angry, thank goodness. However, she also didn't look happy either. More . . . wistful. Like she'd just eaten a sandwich made of regret.

Zeb frowned. "Are you sure we can't play it? Or at least *look* at it?"

After a huge sigh, Grandma Gretchen shook her head. "The game isn't finished. If your Grandpa had had more time, he could have made it worth playing. He was working on it when we lost him." Her voice hitched, and Grandma had to clear her throat.

Ellie's left eye welled up with a pool of tears. "You miss him so much, don't you?"

They all did, but Grandma missed him most. Ellie ducked under the game to put her arms around Grandma's waist. She hugged her tightly.

The phone rang. Grandma sniffled and released Ellie. Then she set the game down and bustled toward the persistent ringing down the hallway in the kitchen.

Ellie looked around the room. "Where's Mr. Grumpy Pants?"

The cat was nowhere in sight. Thank goodness. Maybe Ellie's arm's current mishmash of scratches would have time to heal before the cat added to the scab-fest.

"I don't know." Zeb's voice sounded dead. "Probably catching mice. He's a good mouser."

Fine, maybe the cat had a redeeming quality.

"Well," Ellie said, flumping to the floor, "I guess that's that. No Candy Kingdom for us."

"Uh-huh." Zeb held the game again, eyeing it hungrily. "Er,

PATTERNS

right."

"Are you going to put it back up in that deep, dark corner where Grandma keeps it?"

"I just want one look inside. Grandma didn't say we couldn't look at it. She just said it wasn't finished. As long as we're careful and don't lose any of the pieces, she probably won't mind."

That might be true. Or it might not. Ellie wasn't sure.

"It could be that the game brings back too many memories of Grandpa, and that's why Grandma doesn't want us to play it," Ellie said. Zeb wasn't the only one who could come up with theories.

From the kitchen came a loud gasp. "Oh, no!" Grandma Gretchen's voice echoed all the way to their ears.

Ellie dashed down the hall. Zeb followed close behind.

The phone shook in Grandma's hand. "Mr. Grumpy Pants was hit by a car."

"Oh, no!" Ellie gently took the phone and hung it up for Grandma. "Is he . . . ?"

"That was Phyllis Blankenship next door. She found him. Her husband Ned is already on the way to the veterinarian with Mr. Grumpy Pants. I have to get down there right now." Grandma grabbed her purse off the counter and dug inside it. "Where are my keys?"

"Here they are." Zeb located them on their hook attached to a large, wooden plaque shaped like a rooster. "Do you want us to go with you?"

Tears squeezed from the sides of Grandma Gretchen's eyes. "Without Mr. Grumpy Pants, I'll go crazy in this big, empty house."

"He's gone?" Zeb gasped. "The vet can't do anything?"

"No. I mean, I don't know. Ned and Phyllis don't know if he'll make it."

"You should get down there, Grandma," Ellie said. "We'll be fine here."

Together they shuttled Grandma outside and down the steps toward her car. "I'm old enough to be in charge," Zeb said.

"Yeah, don't worry about us," Ellie said. "We'll just play some games inside."

"That's fine, dears." Grandma tried putting the house key into the car door's lock twice before getting the right key. "I'll come back soon."

With that, she was gone.

Zeb looked at Ellie. "It's too bad about Mr. G. But in the meantime, Ellie, you're a genius."

"I am?"

"The way you said, 'We'll just be playing games inside,' and she agreed." He grinned from ear to ear. "We have permission."

Don't Spin Green

Possibly because the singing might suddenly get much too loud, Ellie stood back. Zeb shimmied the lid off the top of the box. Sure enough, the higher he lifted it, the louder the singing got in Ellie's ears.

"Do you hear that?" she shouted.

"What?" Zeb looked at her weirdly. "I know it makes an unpleasant bumping sound as the cardboard slides, but it can't be helped."

No, not that. "I mean the singing. Kind of like when all the young boys sing together in a stone church with a really high ceiling."

Zeb smirked. "I think they call that *tinnitus*. Ringing in the ears."

"Whatever." Ellie didn't need his smirks. "That's not even a word. And this is *singing*, not ringing." Nevertheless, his snotty remark proved something: Ellie was the only one who could hear the song. Why? Was the game dangerous? Was the song a lure, or was it a warning? "Wait, Zeb. Don't—"

Zeb tugged the lid off the game.

"Wow," they both breathed at the same time. The spinners were golden, with the same high shine as the box's lid. A set of cards was neatly stacked beside a cup filled with some kind of game coins — discs of every color of candy.

"Where's the board? Open the board." Ellie abandoned all hesitation. Now that the box was open, they should see all of it. Zeb unfolded the colorful board with a rainbow of squares on a path and four sections of challenges. "I wonder what the rules are?" Were there written rules? Had Grandpa gotten that far? The game certainly looked complete. Playing pieces — six of them — lay in a cubby. Each piece came in a different color.

"Oh, check it out. These look like Gummo Bears." When Ellie lifted one, she saw that each wore a tiny Valentine conversation heart stamped on its chest. This one, the yellow one, had a white heart with the word "Gretchen" on it.

Gretchen! That was Grandma's first name — on her favorite color.

Ellie picked up another. "Ronald." That was Grandpa Ronny's first name, his whole name. How cute that he'd named the bears after himself and Grandma.

No wonder the game filled Grandma's face with sorrow. Grandma Gretchen must miss him like Ellie and Zeb missed TV.

Okay, possibly even more.

"Look at this!" Zeb said before Ellie got a chance to read the other names on the bears' hearts. "It's . . . a journey game. There's a path and obstacles and a spinner and a bunch of 'luck' cards — see? They've got Lucky Ducks on them." Lucky Ducks were Zeb's favorite chocolate-covered candies. He'd probably eat all the Lucky Ducks in Bremen City if he had the chance.

He turned over a card to show her. "Jump ahead three spaces." He frowned, "Well, that's a kind of boring one." He set it aside, and Ellie picked it up. There was pretty art of a Lucky Duck candy on one side, and words and a picture of a forest of licorice sticks on the other. Zeb took it and showed her a different card. "Cut your enemy off at the knees."

"Cut off your enemy's knees!" Ellie gasped. "That sounds mean. And violent." She tugged it out of Zeb's hand and shoved it back in the stack. "Let's skip this one."

Maybe the creep-factor was actually why Grandma didn't want them playing it. It looked so colorful and innocent at first glance, but it sounded a lot more dangerous when they looked closer.

"Aw, hardly. I mean, look at the board. The enemy is this dude with the maniacal grin over here? He's nothing but a gingerbread boy." Zeb snorted. "How dangerous could a cookie be?"

"Maybe not dangerous, but definitely annoying. You're the one who claimed a person could be bored to death. The fairy tale about the gingerbread boy is my personal proof that someone could potentially be annoyed to death."

Their mother had often read them the story of the cookie who always ran away—at least until the fox ate him.

Zeb's stomach growled. "Let's stop talking about cookies. At this rate, we'll never eat cookies again." He pulled half a raisin cookie from his cargo pants pocket and tucked it into his cheek. "These don't really count as cookies."

"Ew." All this candy talk was getting to Ellie, too. "Let's just see what else is going on in this game." She looked away from his chewing the crumbly, sugarless mass. "If only these candy coins were edible. They look delicious." She lifted a purple-colored candy.

It may have been plastic, but it still had a heavenly, fruity smell of blackberries. The same colors as the Gummo Bears, each different coin emitted a different candy scent: apple for the green coin, cherry for the red, peach for the orange-colored coin, blueberry for the blue, banana for the yellow. Ellie pushed that one away. She'd had too many banana smells for one week already.

"Aha! Here are the rules for setup." Zeb tugged a piece of paper from the box.

"Finally!" Ellie zipped it away from him. "I'll read them, and you set it up. I'm better at reading aloud."

"Fine. Because I'm better at visualizing directions."

Whatever. Ellie scanned the rules. "Give each of us a bear and put it on the starting square."

"What color do you want to be? I call blue because my favorite color is blue, and—hey." Zeb stopped. "My name's on this one."

Ellie put down the rules. "What? Really?"

Zeb sifted through the bears. "This one is named Darla, and another one is named Troy." Their parents' names! One for each of them. "And yours is orange."

Orange? Cool. Ellie's favorite color. "How—?"

"What's next?" Zeb grabbed for the rules, but Ellie snapped them back and started reading again.

"Win by getting to the Candy Court to save Princess Cupcake." Ellie shook her head. She knew exactly what her brother would say next.

"Save the princess? Yes!" Zeb dug through all the playing pieces and cards, making a huge mess. "I gotta see. Is she pretty?"

She was pretty. Ellie relinquished the card featuring Princess Cupcake.

Zeb gazed at the princess with the cupcake-festooned tiara. "Oh, yeah. I'm coming for you, Princess Cupcake."

"You are hopeless." It wasn't that Zeb cared about real-life girls yet. He was only eleven. However, he'd always been a sucker for a game where he could save a princess, like in *Konky Strong*, where the giant lizard steals the princess, and it's up to the lowly lumberjack to save her. Zeb rocked that game. He wasn't half bad at all the *Zenda Prisoner Princess* games, either. "Completely hopeless, my brother."

"I'm not hopeless. I'm hope-*full*." He grinned and held up a new game piece. "Check out these spinners. There are six, so we each get one in our own color." He handed Ellie her orange one with the golden dial.

"Do we take turns or spin at the same time?" She scanned the rules, but there weren't directions for that question. "Otherwise, I'd say it looks pretty straightforward. Spin, move, try not to fall in the traps, get to the castle, save the princess, win. I'll race you to the castle!"

Ellie dropped to her knees beside him and put her orange Gummo Bear on the board's starting space beside Zeb's little blue bear. The spinners had colors, numbers, and one *Draw a Lucky Duck Card* space.

Something about those cards . . . Ellie shivered. Landing on a color or a number first would be better. A glance at the board told her not to land on the color green. Definitely, don't spin green — the first green had a picture of a tunnel, and into the tunnel flowed what looked like a gooey river of chocolate.

It's not that I don't like chocolate. I love it. But . . . does that chocolate kind of look like it's moving? Her eyes were playing tricks on her, just like her ears were. The singing got louder as she lifted her spinner.

"Ready? Set. Spin!" Zeb spun, and Ellie flicked her pointer finger. At exactly the same time, their spinners both landed on — oh, no! Green!

At that very second, the volume of the singing in Ellie's ears cranked to one hundred.

And everything went black.

The Candy Kingdom

"Help!" Ellie bobbed up and down in a murky river. "Help!" She had to keep her head above the surface of the brown sludge to breathe. "Zeb?" Every time she came up for air, she looked everywhere for Zeb, but she couldn't see him.

All she could see was a stone tunnel looming ahead of her, and all she could feel was the swift, powerful current of the heavy, gooey river dragging her toward its dark mouth.

Two seconds ago, she and Zeb had been spinning spinners in the dim yellow room that smelled of Mr. Grumpy Pants and old corn flakes—hadn't they?

Now she was close to drowning in a river of—what was this? She rolled her tongue across her lips.

This wasn't water. This was a chocolate river.

"Zeb?" she hollered again.

"Over here. Give me your hand." Zeb stood on the bank of the river, just at the opening of the tunnel. He was breathing heavily, but her brother was a swim team champ. "I got out upstream.

Quick—we don't know where that tunnel leads."

Swimming through chocolate wasn't like swimming at the Bremen City pool. It was better and worse at the same time. The liquid was heavy, so she didn't sink as fast, but it was also thick—like Grandma Gretchen's stickiest oatmeal.

Ellie reached for Zeb. He tugged, and part of her came out—arms, then torso, then right leg. Finally, Ellie's left leg slurped free of the sticky sludge.

"Where are we?" Ellie looked at the sky, the bushes, the river, the meadow, all more colorful than any amusement park.

"Isn't it obvious? We're in the Candy Kingdom."

What? "You mean we're inside the game?"

"Isn't it obvious?"

Obvious, maybe, but . . . "More like impossible."

"Yes, but how else do you explain it?"

"I don't know." Ellie brushed the chocolate off herself. It came off in dust, the air drying it up fast, wafting it away, not as goo but as cocoa powder. Like chalk dust. Speaking of chalk dust . . . "Hey! I read about something like this in *Mary Poppins*. Mary and Burt and the children jumped into a chalk painting and danced with cartoon penguins." If Mary could do it, maybe jumping into a board game wasn't so far-fetched. Plus, they dusted themselves off when they came out of the chalk drawing. "Maybe it's similar to our transporting in Grandpa's game. But without the cartoon penguins."

"Sounds legit." Zeb didn't seem to have any problem with their situation. "Come on."

But what had caused their leap into Candy Kingdom?

Zeb dusted himself, too, as they walked up a trail through an

expanse of meadow. Meadow, yes, but with little mounds of green bushes that looked suspiciously like Grandma Gretchen's boxes of corn-flake wreaths. Dots of color grew between them—bright and sweet. This place didn't grow flowers. It grew Sparklies, Glinties, and Shinies.

"You want to know how we got here? Well, naturally, I have a theory." Naturally. "When we spun, and both landed on green, *bam!* The magic of the game sucked us inside."

Obviously. "But I wish I knew how," Ellie said.

"I haven't worked out that detail yet. Besides, who cares how? We're here!" Zeb grabbed Ellie's hand and pulled her up the embankment to a path made of pretty rocks and waved his hand at the dazzling world. "And *here* is so much better than any cat's bedroom."

Ellie could not argue with that, but a strong worry nagged at her. "How do we go back?"

"Who cares?" Zeb reached down and snapped a petal off a flower. "This world tastes a million times better than raisin cookies." He stuffed part of the petal in his mouth and handed part to Ellie. She tested it against her tongue. Sugar cookie with cherry frosting, her favorite!

For the first time, Ellie started to really open her eyes to where she'd landed. A sky as blue as a blue-raspberry slushie capped over them in a dome dotted with spun cotton candy clouds of both blue and pink. Patches of land near and far were studded with red and black licorice-stick-tree forests. *Just like on the Lucky Duck Card.* She shivered.

"Check out the sun!" It was just like the art on the game board—what little she'd seen of it before the flash trip into the game. "Is it a butterscotch candy?" If so, it was a butterscotch candy that glowed and could warm the air—plus make it smell sweeter than any stale banana.

Zeb climbed a little rise in the stony pathway. It led to a bridge made of cobblestones. "Check it out. The bridge's stones look like rocks, but I'd bet good money they are those chocolate rocks like Gordo McTwigg got in a goodie bag from his cousin's birthday party."

Ellie came up beside Zeb. "So, this is the game Grandpa made." Wow. Amazing, but also sad. "Too bad he couldn't see inside this place himself."

"Aw, sure he could. If he imagined it, it was inside him all the time—and he was thereby inside it." Zeb and his theories and philosophies. "Come on. I smell doughnuts."

If there was one thing Zeb couldn't resist, it was a doughnut. Ellie didn't even bother trying to stop him from chasing the scent. However, Zeb halted, frowning. "I wish I'd taken a better look at the game board before we jumped. I only saw the first quadrant."

"Me, too. It was so pretty."

"No, I mean so we'd at least have a mental map of this place."

"Oh, right." Good point. "We probably each noticed different things. Maybe we could each say what we remember and try to piece it together."

"Like a puzzle? Yeah. You're good at puzzles."

"No, Grandma Gretchen is good at puzzles. I'm fair to middling."

"Point taken, but you're not bad."

Zeb was complimenting her? Well, hand Ellie her diary and a pen to note down this momentous day.

Oh, her diary. It was back at Grandma Gretchen's house.

Are we ever going to get back there? What about Grandma? Would she wonder what had happened to them? They'd been in this place for half an hour already. Grandma might return from the veterinarian at any moment. Could Ellie and Zeb make it back in time to meet her? Or would she just find the game scattered around and call the police for a search and rescue party?

And what about Mom and Dad? What would happen when they found out Zeb and Ellie were missing?

This was awful. They were inconsiderate. Choosing to play this game might have terrible consequences for people they love.

"Zeb, I'm afraid Grandma will be worried if we aren't back when she gets home."

Zeb looked at his watch. "Quit being a worrywart. We've only been here for about a minute, according to my watch." But who was counting?

"Are you sure your watch wasn't damaged by the chocolate river?"

He lifted it to his ear. "It's ticking. We're *fine*."

Ellie wasn't convinced. "Have you thought about *how* we're going to get back?"

"Standing around here isn't going to tell us anything."

Well, at least that much was clear.

"Come on." Zeb patted the wall of the bridge and marched down the far side. "I want to see more of the Candy Kingdom. It makes me think of Grandpa Ronny."

"Wait for me." Ellie had to jog to keep up. Zeb's legs were longer than hers. "So, hey. Do you think if we follow the path to the end, we can get home?"

Zeb slowed up a little, and Ellie caught her breath. "That does sound logical. Save the princess, beat the game, get the trophy—that's usually the way of things."

None of those rewards involved going home, unfortunately. "It seems like our best option. Wasn't there a castle at the end?"

"With a princess." Zeb moved his eyebrows up and down. "I've got to see her."

Ellie wanted to think the castle was the portal back to Grandma's house, but of course, there was no evidence on which to base that wish. "Let's go to the castle." They didn't have any better guess. "Besides, the game's rules said go to the candy court and save the princess to win the game."

"Great. The castle probably has a royal kitchen, and I'm starving. No matter what Grandpa's watch says, my internal clock says it's lunchtime already." Zeb's internal clock always signaled mealtime. "You think there are any doughnuts to eat around here?"

"Doughnuts for lunch? The second Mom's not watching . . ."

"Excuse me?" A thin, stringy voice bounced into Ellie's ears, and she looked up to see a thin, stringy creature, like a fat shoelace in a pile—except with a face, big eyes with dark eyelashes. The air all around the creature wafted with the scent of fried dough. "I'm Funny."

At Your Service

It could speak! Ellie gasped and jumped a half-step backward. There were living creatures in this place! She'd caught a brief glance of characters on a couple of the Lucky Duck cards, but she hadn't dreamed they'd be alive—or able to talk.

"Um, you're *funny*?" Zeb asked the dough and then sniff-laughed. "Lots of people think they're amusing when they're not, though."

"Zeb. Don't be rude." Ellie shoved him.

"No, it's my name. Funny the Funnel Cake." She bowed. "At your service."

Funnel cake? Wasn't that a treat Grandpa Ronny had bought for Zeb and Ellie to share when they went to the county fair? The food truck lady had poured some kind of cake batter through a funnel and drizzled it into a vat of hot oil. It had fried right before their eyes, and then the lady had scooped it all out onto a plate and dusted it with powdered sugar. Mmm. Now Ellie was the one getting hungry, just at the memory of the fun day with Grandpa Ronny.

"Nice to meet you, Funny." Ellie bowed in return, even if it was weird to bow to a stringy pile of fried dough with eyes and spindly bits of dough for legs and arms, a thicker swirl for its body. "I'm Ellie, and this is my brother Zeb."

Funny jumped. "Like the Gummo Bear royalty!" Her eyes widened. "Were you named for them?"

Ellie shifted her weight. It was probably better not to admit that the bears were likely named for her and Zeb. Funny held a bucket in each hand, brimming with what looked like the chocolate from the river.

"We're looking for the doughnuts." Zeb rubbed his belly.

Talk about awkwardness! Zeb basically just asked to eat Funny or her sisters, or her cousins, or whatever. Ellie must have looked horrified.

Luckily, Funny just laughed. "It's okay, Friend Ellie. Doughnuts are my food, not my family. In fact, chocolate-drizzled doughnuts are the only thing we eat. You are what you eat, hee-hee." Her laugh twinkled like a bell.

"Good. Let's get going!" Zeb marched down the path. "My nose can lead the way. It knows doughnuts anywhere."

Funny let out a shrill cry. "Oh, no. Not over the chocolate rock bridges." Before Zeb could gloat about being right about the cobblestones, Funny said, "Jinja and his army have their roadblock set up at the bridge to Lake Cocoa. We need to go through the Cinnamon Mists instead. Oh, but you don't have gas masks. Your eyes and noses will sting from the spice."

Ellie's mind swirled. "Gas masks!"

Funny's shoulders fell. "It's our only choice these days. If we want chocolate glaze for our doughnuts—and we definitely do because it keeps us healthy—we can't use Lake Cocoa anymore. We have to brave the Cinnamon Mists on our land's border to get upstream to collect it from the river. The Mists are dangerous, but they serve two purposes: to keep us in and to keep our enemies out."

"Chocolate glaze is someone's health food! See?" But then Zeb frowned as if the problems in Funny's situation finally dawned on him. "You're saying you can't get to your nutrition because of this Jinja guy? That is so wrong! And you have to go through poisonous mists? Who let this Jinja and his army into the kingdom? Let me at them! Anybody who messes with a person's chocolate glazed doughnuts deserves a beating."

Aw, Zeb had never beaten up anyone or anything in his life, except in a video game. *Say, this was kind of like the most realistic VR video game of all time.*

"What my brother is saying with so much enthusiasm is that we wish we knew how to help." In no way could Ellie and Zeb stop a scary army and a bad guy with a name like Jinja. What was he—a ninja or something? Ellie and Zeb had never even signed up for karate classes. They would have had to miss *Grunting for Money* if they went to karate practice. "We're actually trying to find a way down the path ourselves."

"Where are you trying to go?" Funny asked as they passed a haystack made of frosted wheat bricks, just like that box from Grandma's craft pile. "Candy Castle to see Princess Cupcake?" She sighed. "That seems like all anybody ever wants to do."

"So, she's at the castle!" Zeb's eyes lit up with Princess Interest again. "I mean, yes and no. Much as I'd love to get to the castle and save the princess, we probably ought to go home."

Ellie sighed in relief. So, Zeb *did* realize that Grandma would be worried.

"Oh, good! Because once you save Princess Cupcake, she can save you."

It's Not a Game, It's War

Zeb's jaw dropped onto his chest. If he'd been holding a chocolate doughnut, he would have dropped it, too. "She saves us? What do you mean?"

Ellie wondered that, too. "Yeah, Funny. In all the other games out there, the player saves the princess."

"Yeah, and then the winner gets a trophy."

Ugh. Zeb and his trophy obsession.

"What other games? What's a game?" Funny laughed. "You mean like Jinja's army blocking our only pathway to Lake Cocoa and Candy Castle? Because that's not a game. It's war."

The word must have caught Zeb's attention. "You're at war?"

"Uh, hello. Gas masks?" Funny coiled and sprang and pointed at a pink wall of fog in front of them.

The Cinnamon Mists! Teensy red water droplets filled the air across a blurry meadow so thick they couldn't see more than ten feet. Ellie had to squint and cover her nose to keep out the fog's strong scent. Zeb sniffled and rubbed at his eyes.

"Ouch! That stings!" Ellie smashed her palms over her eyes, which were crying involuntarily. "I can't even breathe!" She started coughing and turned her back, covering her face with her jacket's sleeve.

"We can't go in there," she told Zeb. "Not without protection." He turned to Funny. "You have to get that chocolate back to your house, but we can't go with you. Will you be safe in the fog?"

Funny shrugged. "The gas masks help, as long as I don't slip into one of the chasms." There were chasms, too? Oh, dear. "We lost one of my sisters that way. Now, collecting the chocolate from the river upstream is my job." She shrugged, and the chocolate in the bucket sloshed. "I have to. For my family."

"What about your parents?" Ellie asked.

"My mother protects the little ones, and Father is running the war."

Running the war! They had to do something. They couldn't just say, *Nice to meet you. Well, okay. Bye. Good luck with your war.*

"Zeb," Ellie whispered. "We've got to help. Funny shouldn't have to risk her life and cross this dangerous area just for their daily needs. Somebody has to stop Jinja."

"And his army?" Funny laughed drily. "You two? You're kids like me. All the Funnel People together couldn't *begin* to stop Jinja's army. He has too many troops."

Ellie pictured the army: tall soldiers, guns in hand, heavy boots, straight lines. Yikes. She and Zeb couldn't do anything against that kind of strength. They were kids. All they had was . . .

Ellie checked her pockets and found—not much. A dime, a big piece of folded aluminum foil from the raisin cookie project, a folded piece of paper, and a magnifying glass from when she

was counting stitches on one of the knitting projects — and in case Grandma had let her look at the puzzle closet again.

Zeb's jaw was set. "We're not going to leave you in this danger. Someone's messing with your food supply. You lost your sister. That's not cool."

Ellie's chest clutched. It almost sounded like Zeb cared about sisters.

"Yeah." Ellie echoed him and then suddenly second-guessed herself. What were they thinking? If they died in here, they'd never get out, and then Grandma's heart would break, not to mention Mom and Dad's, because they'd have no idea what happened to their kids.

Well, if Zeb intended to go up against an army, Ellie intended to at least keep the two of them alive.

Mixed-up Map

"Thank you, Friend Ellie and Friend Zeb. I appreciate the sentiment. Many Lucky Ducks to you for it." She bowed and turned to go, but she didn't express confidence that Ellie and Zeb could succeed. "Farewell for now."

Funny looked downright weird with the gas mask on, but she set off through the Cinnamon Mists. Would she be all right?

Ellie should go with her — but she couldn't brave that stinging fog. There was no way. It was toxic! *Bye, Funny. Be safe.*

"What in the world can we do to help her?" Ellie asked, turning to Zeb — but he wasn't beside her.

He had set off marching down the road, past a pile of boulders.

No, wait. Those weren't boulders. They were stacks of dried apples with faces carved in them — just like in Grandma Gretchen's cat room — but they looked like an avalanche instead.

"Wait up." Ellie jogged to reach him. "What are you planning to do?"

"I'm going to have a talk with this Jinja dude. Tell him to quit hogging the bridge."

Oh, great. Zeb thought he could negotiate with a bridge-blocking villain? Make that a villain with an army. Ellie's heart pounded, and not from the jogging.

"You're going to put Funny"—*and us*—"in danger."

Zeb didn't respond. They crossed another bridge over the chocolate stream and headed toward the black- and red-licorice-stick hills where the path curved out of sight.

"Do we have any idea how this will go down?" Ellie knew she sounded like she was trying to be too grown-up, but this could be grown-up peril. "I'm worried. We should think this through. At least stop, and we can put together our map. You know, like we said."

This got Zeb to slow down. He turned to her. "Yeah, okay." Looking across the landscape dotted with cornflake sculptured shrubbery and dried apple head boulders, they found a spot to sit down.

"What do you remember?" Ellie pulled a piece of paper from her pocket. It was Grandma Gretchen's chore list for her from this morning. She picked a blade of grass. She'd used one to draw on the sidewalk at Grandma's last summer, so it might work. She rubbed it against the paper. It did work—but it made her fingers sticky. "Hey. This is candy grass!"

With thumb and forefinger, Zeb plucked a blade and stuck it in his mouth. "Spearmint. Refreshing."

Ellie tasted it, too. Yuck. While it might be refreshing as a breath mint, it definitely shouldn't count as candy. Ellie spit hers out.

"There was the path, and it went something like this." Zeb traced his finger in a snake-like pattern on the paper through the four quadrants. "And I remember the Spearmint Hills—here."

"But that's where the Cinnamon Mists are supposed to be."

"No. I didn't see those on the game board. I *know* that section said Spearmint Hills."

Ellie shook her head. He might have it jumbled in his mind. After all, he did only see it for a few seconds before they spun their dials and got whooshed inside here. "Now, I remember the path. It was almost just like you said. And the chocolate river on this green space. And the Licorice Stick Forest . . ."

"You're getting it wrong. The hills are over here. See?"

"Zeb—"

"Here. Let me." He grabbed the paper from Ellie's hand and took over the drawing.

"Whatever. It's our only piece of paper, and you're wrecking—hey. That's actually pretty good." Ellie sat up on her knees and looked over Zeb's drawing. It wasn't a very detailed picture—since he only had a stub of green grass to use as a pencil—but the elements of the game board all appeared as she'd seen it. And he was right: the hills were over on the other side.

"How did you do that?" Ellie marveled at it, taking it from his hands and studying it. Sure enough, no Cinnamon Mists, but a meadow instead. "I don't get it. Are you magical or something?"

"It's not the whole game board, just the upper left quadrant."

"But still! It's amazing. How did you do that?"

"I guess I see things, and then I remember them. My brain takes a picture, I think." He shrugged one shoulder. "It's how I can't forget facts about ringing in the ears, or words like *theoretical* or *ratio*. Sometimes I wish I could."

"Well, it came in pretty handy today. This is golden!" Ellie punched Zeb in the shoulder, but in a nice way. "I get it. That's the

bridge by the lake. We're not that far away."

"Right? Let's go and at least check it out."

"Okay, but can we go quickly?" Ellie started jogging, her feet clunking against the chocolate rocks along the path they'd mapped out to the bridge.

"You in a big hurry or something?" Zeb glanced at his watch. "It's only been fifteen minutes since we got here."

"Fifteen minutes! Look at the sun, Zeb. It's getting to be late afternoon, almost sunset. Grandma will explode with worry when she sees we're gone, and all there is on the floor is a bunch of game pieces of a game she told us specifically not to play."

"You're such a worrier. I'm telling you, this watch *never* fails."

"Unless you forget to wind it."

"I didn't forget. I never forget." Zeb got quiet. "It'd be like forgetting Grandpa Ronny."

Oh. Right. Zeb wouldn't forget. Neither could Ellie. Grandpa Ronny was all hugs and smiles and a piece of candy in his cargo pants pocket for her.

"Fine. I won't argue anymore." Not because she was wrong about the time of day, but because arguing wasted time — time they would need to figure out how to get home.

After they helped Funny and her family. *After* they defeated Jinja and his army.

Right.

Ooh, and there it was! The army loomed at the bridge, like a gooey yellow and purple terror.

Gooey Terror

Ellie skidded to a halt on the path. All the saliva in her mouth turned to ashes.

Zeb nearly collided with her when he stopped, but then his jaw fell open, and he said, "When Funny said *army*, I never pictured anything this sticky."

"Or this terrifying," Ellie squeaked.

About a soccer field away stood a battalion of soldiers nearly as wide as the lake. In perfect rows, with blank expressions, and fierce in purple and yellow—

"Are those army guys *marshmallow*?" Zeb said, tugging her behind some corn-flake shrubbery so they could watch unnoticed. "They are. They're Marshmallow Pips!" A gurgling, stifled scream roiled in his throat.

"Honestly, Zeb, I never thought a bunny, or a baby chicken could look so menacing. Do you see their dead eyes?"

Zeb plopped down on the ground. "If there were only a few of them, it'd be easy. We could get them with these." From his

pocket down on the side of his cargo pants, he took out a half-dozen petrified raisin cookies.

"What? Why do you have those? And what good would raisin cookies do against a marshmallow army?"

"To answer your first question, I thought I might need a snack."

"Zeb! Those are so gross, though."

"I'm a boy. I need food. I don't have a discerning palate."

"You and your big words."

"What I meant to extract from my pocket was this." Zeb tugged out the rose-trimming shears. "We could — I don't know — stab the Pips if they weren't fresh."

Ellie squinted to see across the meadow at their foes. "They do look fresh. But why would freshness matter?"

"In fresh marshmallow, rose-trimming shears will only goosh into the goo and get lost in the gloppy heart of the first marshmallow we try to attack."

Ugh. Too true. So gloppy. They stood up again and studied the legion of marshmallow animals.

"Then what weapon could hurt them? They're indestructible." That undeniable fact terrified her most. "And don't look at me to eat them all, please."

"No, I wouldn't wish that on someone who can't even enjoy a good raisin cookie." He took a dry bite, then wrinkled his nose in thought. "You see Jinja anywhere?"

"Nope." Not that she knew what to look for. Ellie only saw yellow and purple — a vast sea of at least five hundred puffy bodies and one black eye painted on either side of the chickens' and bunnies' heads. "If only we had a death ray."

"Yeah. Like Captain Firestarter. He always has a death ray."

Zeb pulled the invisible trigger on his invisible death ray.

"Unfortunately, this isn't Captain Firestarter's world. This is Candy Kingdom."

"Yeah." Zeb heaved a sigh. "There might be mists of stinging cinnamon juice, but it isn't exactly laser headquarters."

"Too bad Grandpa didn't have a science fiction hobby, too."

"Hey!" Zeb grabbed at Ellie's jacket. "Give me this thing of yours. I need to look in its crevices." He yanked it off her shoulder.

"Knock it off. That's my jacket." Not like it was cold here, but jackets were safe. Going jacketless, well—she just wanted her jacket. "Give it back."

"You got to see the useless loot I brought. Maybe you've got something better." He shook the jacket upside down, and nothing happened. Ellie snatched it back and showed him how the pockets were zipped shut.

From the first pocket, she extracted the dime.

Zeb smirked, annoyed. "Ten cents. Not even a quarter for a gum machine!"

"Not like you brought anything better."

"Sorry." He stuck it in his own pocket, the thief. "Might come in handy. What else have you got in there?"

Ellie tugged out the other two items: the aluminum foil from the cookie project and the magnifying glass from the stitchery project. "Pretty useless, too," she said, huffing a sigh. "We're just two kids with nothing but tinfoil, pruning shears, a magnifying glass, and ten cents. It's useless. And now I can't find the map we drew on the chores list." It must have dropped. "We're never going to be able to help Funny, and her family regain access to their food supply. They'll be stuck walking through those dangerous mists, almost dying every time they're hungry. She's already lost a sister down a chasm!" Tears stung at Ellie's eyes, and not just from remembering the pungent fog. Ellie had lost Grandpa Ronny, and her life hadn't been the same ever again—and she'd only ever seen him in the summers. Poor Funny!

If only Ellie could help. But she couldn't. No one could protect Funny's family. And who would die next? Maybe Funny herself. *Likely* Funny herself. She was the one crossing the Cinnamon Mists every day, facing death.

Ellie's heart cracked like the breaking of peanut brittle.

"Zeb, it's just so sad." But when Ellie looked up, Zeb didn't look the least bit sad. In fact, he was grinning ear to ear, and his eye had a twinkle just like Grandma Gretchen's when she talked about her puzzles. "What? What are you smiling about? This is terrible. Did you *see* all those Pips? How can you not feel the tragedy here?"

Instead of answering, he started singing—the worst nursery rhyme ever.

"The old gray mare just ain't what she used to be
Ain't what she used to be
Ain't what she used to be
The old gray mare just ain't what she used to be
Many long years ago."

Then he laughed like a maniac—before cupping a hand over his mouth and glancing to see whether the army had heard or noticed him. They hadn't.

"You've got to stop that, Zeb."

"What? No way. In fact, I'm starting over." He cleared his

throat and sang it again, and this time with even worse lyrics, which should have been impossible!

"We all know frogs go pop in the microwave,
Pop in the microwave, pop in the microwave.
We all know frogs go pop in the microwave
When you turn it on."

"Zeb, that is disgusting! Stop now." She made a fist and held it in front of his nose. "We have a crisis here, and you're singing terrible Prairie Dog Scout Camp songs?" He'd been a Prairie Pup a couple of summers ago and came home from camp with a host of truly revolting songs, apparently including that one. "Wake up! Let's do what we can to help the Funnel People."

"Fine. But it's your fault. You started my brain thinking when you said you wished we had a death ray."

"Captain Firestarter always has a death ray." Ellie looked at the sky as if a blue slushie would somehow have their answer. "Pew, pew! Brrzzzt!" She aimed her own imaginary death ray at the silent dome above.

"Right! You're a genius."

"I am?"

"Fine, maybe *I* am the genius. But you sparked my genius, so I'm giving you some credit. Don't get too used to it."

She wouldn't. "Just tell me what you're talking about."

Instead of telling her, he laid out the items from her pocket and *showed* her his ingenious plan.

Pop in the Microwave

With careful hands, Zeb unfolded the piece of aluminum foil. "It's nice and long," he said, smoothing out the wrinkles. "This is totally going to work."

"What is going to work? What are you doing?" Ellie thought maybe he had gone a little crazy. Maybe the chocolate river they'd fallen into was poisonous, and it had a brain-eating virus in it, and it was only a matter of time before they were *both* as loony as Zeb seemed right now.

"Hand me your magnifying glass."

She did. Zeb tilted it carefully back and forth above the tinfoil. Every couple of seconds, the reflection would catch the sun and send a blinding glare into her eyes.

"Ouch. Zeb!" She put up a hand to shield her vision.

"See? It works!"

Yep, he'd gone crazy—totally *gone 'round the bend*, as Grandma Gretchen would say.

"It's awesome." Zeb jumped up and refolded the aluminum

foil carefully. "We've totally got them now!"

"Uh, Zeb?" Ellie hated to break it to him, but if Candy Kingdom had a place for the insane, he was in danger of getting locked up there for a long time. "Are you feeling all right?"

"Never better. Come on. Let's find some high ground."

"Uh, okay." She followed along but with dragging feet. "I don't know what we're planning here. We don't have a microwave, or a frog, or Captain Firestarter's death ray."

"Uh, hello! What we have here will do just fine." He patted the foil and the magnifying glass as they climbed a hill topped with dried apple boulders. "Reflective technology will be just as effective as a death ray."

Reflective technology? Then it came clear to her. "We all know *Pips* go pop in the microwave!" she shouted and then started to laugh. Quickly she shushed herself because they might be within earshot of the Pips. Except . . . could Pips hear? They didn't have ears or anything.

Wait, the bunnies had ears — long ones. Ellie and Zeb had better keep quiet.

From atop an overlooking hill, they surveyed the area and the enemy. This location was still too far away for an attack.

"If we can get to that next hill," — Zeb pointed across an open meadow — "it will have the perfect vantage point for my plan."

Running in the wide open, where they could be seen, was dangerous. "I don't know." Ellie looked both ways. "Will they spot us? And attack?"

"Trust me," Zeb said.

Trust him? Did she? Ellie hadn't ever asked herself this question before. Did she *trust* her brother? He'd been sporadically horrible to her for her whole life—just like all big brothers. He'd told her to give him five, and then he'd pulled his hand away and told her she was too slow. He'd colored on her homework. He'd changed the channel when she was watching *Polly's Townhouse Friends* and refused to change it back.

Zeb had been the bane of her existence much of her nine years of life.

"Please?" Zeb said, tugging her arm. "I'll keep you safe. I promise. Trust me just this once?"

Ellie gritted her teeth. "Okay."

He smiled and darted down the hill from their hiding place. "We'll go on our bellies through the tall grass. They'll never see us." He flopped down on his tummy and began to crawl. Sure enough, the grass blades didn't swish as he made his way through them.

Ellie crouched down and followed the trail he'd blazed through the grass. Soon they were at the backside of the ideal hill. "You were right."

"Thanks for trusting me." Zeb took her hand and helped her over a dried-apple-head boulder. "Come on. We're almost there."

Ellie huffed and puffed her way to the top of the tall hill, where she saw their enemy in full array: row after row—purple then yellow, purple then yellow—stood at vacant attention. Eerie. "Let's get to work," she said.

"If I can just . . ." Zeb tilted the magnifying glass, while Ellie held the foil. "Tip it this way a bit. Yes!" he whispered. "That's it!"

"Keep it steady," Ellie urged.

Zeb focused the light from the butterscotch-disc-sun onto the foil, which Ellie then sent reflecting in the direction of the Pips army.

Across the distance, a broad glint from the foil lightened up a

row of ten or so Pips.

"Now, just be patient. This will work, I'm sure of it."

It didn't happen immediately. Zeb's watch ticked loudly. Ellie's arm grew tired. But then, something started to happen.

"Am I imagining that"—Zeb jutted his chin, still holding his aim firm—"or are they growing?"

Ellie shook her head. "It's real. I see it, too." Zeb's plan was pretty boss. "Reflective technology. I understand now." Sort of.

Little by little, the row of purple bunny soldiers expanded, first their heads and ears, then their puffy bodies. Puff, puff, puff—soon, they were five times their original size.

"I get that we're puffing them up, but how will we know when they're defeated?" For now, they just looked bigger. And scarier. Giant marshmallow soldiers waiting to attack.

"Now!" Zeb dropped his magnifying glass, and Ellie let her arms go limp. Oh, how they ached. "Look!" He pointed, and sure enough, something happened.

Holy macaroni Kleenex boxes, spray-painted gold. "They're deflating!"

A long hissing sound rose through the afternoon air as the bunny Pips shrank, and shrank, and shrank. The whole front line of them fell limp in a puddle of white and purple goo.

"It worked, Zeb. It really worked!"

"Quick, aim at the next line." He held up his magnifying glass and helped Ellie angle the foil's reflection onto a new row of troops—yellow chicks this time. Soon, they began puffing up, too.

Their brief rest and the surge of excitement had healed Ellie's arms. "Let me at them!" Together they could laser blast every single alternating row of pastel Pips. After a bit, they removed the reflected beam and—*hiss!* The second row of Jinja's army deflated to a white and yellow pool on the rocky ground.

The next row of Pips behind their fallen clones made no sign they'd noticed the loss. Maybe they couldn't see it.

Zeb was giddy with excitement. "Two rows down, about twenty to go."

"We'd better hurry. It won't stay daylight here forever." And maybe Candy Kingdom became more dangerous at night. "In fact." Oh, no. The sun was about to sink. "We've only got about a minute left before it sets."

With twenty rows to go and no sun to use their reflective technology death ray, they were in big trouble.

A snort echoed through the air. Zeb jerked his head toward it. "What's that?"

Red clouds billowed from a boat's smokestack as it chugged across the lake at high speed. It slid up on the shore, and the lines of Pips parted while a lean, mean, flat figure stepped from the deck of the motorboat. His shout carried over the field of Pips.

"Hold the bridge!"

The Pips fell back into line, filling in the spots where their fellow marshmallows were now nothing but light purple glops of stickiness.

"That must be Jinja," Ellie said. The badness emanated from him, like stink off a pile of composting banana peels and rutabagas. "And look. He's not a ninja, after all. He's a gingerbread man." A tall gingerbread man with an icing-drawn frown and angry eyebrows. "Just like on the game board!"

Why hadn't they thought of that? He'd been right before their eyes when they saw Grandpa's game.

Everything else in this Candy Kingdom had been edible—or

at least looked edible—but not Jinja. He looked like the kind of cookie that left you with stomach distress for a week if you ate it.

Every word of his angry rant penetrated the air. "Useless! If you can't even intimidate our enemies, you're useless. My spies have reported mass movement among the Funnels in the last hour." He paced in front of them and then shouted, "Hold this bridge or be roasted!"

The bunny Pips straightened their ears. The baby chick Pips stretched their necks upward to a surprising and creepy length.

"Why does he want the bridge so much?" Ellie asked Zeb. "Just out of spite?"

"Spite may be right." A voice came from behind them.

"Funny. What are you doing here?" Ellie asked.

"We heard about your attack on the Pips," said a larger funnel cake who might be Funny's dad. "Ingenious. Wish we'd thought of that months ago. Then our children wouldn't have starved for doughnut icing from the chocolate river all this time."

"When you came," Funny said, "I felt hope for the first time. I told my family about your courage, and that you'd said you were going to fight Jinja." Behind Funny and her dad, dozens and dozens of funnel cakes, all similar to Funny, stood shoulder to shoulder. "We couldn't let you fight alone."

"We know how to dispense with the Pips," said Zeb, "but not while the sun is down." He frowned. "Using this technology, we can't exactly do anything until morning."

"We don't have until morning." Funny smiled sadly. "The Pips are receiving Jinja's command to attack even as we speak."

"We're helpless until we have sun." Ellie frowned and looked at her magnifying glass and aluminum foil.

Funny shook her head. "My dad has a question."

The bigger funnel cake stepped forward. "You're humans," he said. Nice of him to notice. His voice was still squeaky but lower than Funny's. "How does the Cinnamon Mist affect you?"

"It burns our eyes." Ellie shuddered at the memory.

"I see," Funny's dad said, nodding.

"And" — Zeb jumped to attention — "our skin! This reminds me of something we tried in my science lab last year when we studied acids."

"Yes!" Ellie gasped. "If it burns human skin, imagine what it could do to the delicate surface of a marshmallow Pip!"

"You're getting the idea," Funny's dad said.

"So, we're going to assault them with oil?" Ellie pictured getting close enough to pour oil on Jinja's soldiers. No, thank you.

"Precisely my plan." Funny's dad led her and Zeb down the hill, and toward a cart the funnel cake army was protecting.

"But how?" The Pips could gloop her to death, and that would be a far inferior way of dying, compared to merely being bored to death at Grandma Gretchen's without television.

Oh, Grandma!

Inside the cart were canisters with pumps, like the kind she and Zeb had used to spray that blue Liquid Miracle Fertilizer on the flowers at Grandma's house.

"I'm sure Funny informed you. The Cinnamon Mists are Jinja's idea of a prison wall." Funny's dad handed each of them a mask and a canister. He showed them how to hoist it on their shoulders and how to secure the masks. "He placed them there to keep full control of the chocolate river so that no one else could access it. There used to be a broad expanse of Minty Meadows. Now it's a toxic rain shower, both day and night. We can't leave our lands, and our people are starving."

Zeb looked ready for war. Nothing got him angrier than when he was hungry, and the thought of someone else going hungry, especially when it wasn't necessary, triggered his fighting instincts. He sniffed the canister. "How did you get concentrated cinnamon oil?"

"We've been scraping it up after it settles on the meadows in the mornings." The two strings of dough that made up his mouth pressed into a flat line. "We then collect it in rain barrels. Jinja didn't know because his spies couldn't enter the fog."

"I get it!" Zeb's eyes lit up, and he shook his canister. "We're going to re-nebulize it!"

Nebulize? Zeb must have seen the confusion on Ellie's face because next, he said, "Turn it into a spray, and use it to melt the Pips."

"We don't even have to touch them?" Whew. Ellie exhaled.

It would work! The funnel cake children had gone without food long enough. Not to mention facing loss in the fog and the chasms! Ellie donned her gas mask and shouldered her canister.

Until . . .

"But, Mr. Funnel," Ellie asked, "what will Jinja do when he sees us coming?"

"He'll try to drown you in Lake Cocoa." Funny said this like it was no big deal, but Ellie had choked on the chocolate river when she landed in Candy Kingdom. The possibility of drowning in it was no joke. "He will order the Pips to surround you and press you into the lake."

Ellie climbed the hill again. She peeked over its top to see the far field where the Pips stood guard. Never had marshmallows looked so sinister.

Yes, sinister. Zeb would be proud of that word, but Ellie wasn't. She was scared. Ellie and Zeb locked gazes.

"Don't be scared, Ellie. Grandpa wouldn't want the characters in his game to be this cruel to the funnel cake children — or any children, for that matter. We have to stop them. We are going to win."

Slowly, she began to believe him. With a little more courage to do what was right, even though it was scary, Ellie slid the mask over her mouth and nose. She tugged the strap of her can of cinnamon oil higher onto her shoulder.

"Ready?" she looked at Zeb.

"Set." Zeb looked at Funny's dad.

"Go!" Ellie sounded the charge, and Zeb led the way. From behind them, hundreds of little feet pounded against the cobblestones of the path, tap-tap-tap! Ellie ran as hard as she could, and too soon, she was at the front lines.

Taste Your Own Cough Medicine

"Fire!" came the call when they were close enough to the Pips' front lines.

Ellie pumped her canister and aimed its nozzle at the first line of marshmallow chicks. A fine spray of oil came out. Even through the mask, Ellie could smell its spicy sting.

"It's working!" Zeb's voice hollered over the sound of the pounding feet on the turf. "They're melting away."

As each tiny drop of spray touched a puffy body, a crater formed, sinking down into the sugar of the surface. "It's disintegrating them," Ellie said, taking one of Zeb's kind of words.

In no time, they were through the first ten rows of troops. The Pips were no match for the power of cinnamon oil.

Zeb hollered, "The oily rainfall doesn't bother Funny or her type because their surfaces are dough and not sugar." He pumped three more times to get pressure in his canister and sprayed another line of bunnies. "But the Pips are melting."

It reminded Ellie of the witch in *The Wizard of Oz*, the way the

Pips' heads sank into their shoulders, their shoulders sank into their torsos, and their torsos sank into their feet.

Three more rows dissolved. They were halfway to the bridge now, and pressing forward fast.

"Taste your own cough medicine, Jinja! How do you like that, eh?" Funny's dad hollered over top of the Pips' heads. "This will teach you to keep all the resources to yourself."

Funny's dad led his few good funnel men across the bridge with their cinnamon spray, vanquishing the Pips, row by row.

"Brandish it at them!" he shouted to his troops, who aimed the spray and let the chicks and bunnies have it.

The chicks' necks stretched. Some clucked. Others screamed.

"I didn't know chickens could scream." Ellie covered her ears to block the disturbing sound.

"They can," Zeb said. Ellie would hear more about why later, but for now, they watched the whole army of yellow marshmallow chicks marching a swift retreat toward the hills. A sea of bunny ears bobbed as the purple creatures bounded away in perfect lines, faster than any marshmallow ought to move.

When all the Pips had disappeared at last, Ellie scanned the horizon for their leader. "Where's Jinja?"

"Look." Zeb pointed. Over a dim green hill, they saw the top of his crispy cookie head disappearing. "Cowards run."

Funny's dad walked up beside them and removed his gas mask. "And the courageous ones fight," he said, and then he bowed to them. "You two gave us courage — and you gave us back our access to Lake Cocoa." He bowed to them. "Thank you."

"We wish we could help you get back Funny's sister." Ellie bowed in return. "I can't imagine what that must be like."

"Yeah, I agree." Zeb looked at Ellie. "Sisters are important."

Ellie's stomach warmed.

"I prefer to suppose she's still out there somewhere." Funny's dad gazed across Lake Cocoa at a far-off island jutting out of the chocolate surface. "Gone for now, but not gone forever."

"You believe that?" Ellie asked. If only that could be true of Grandpa Ronny, and he wasn't really gone forever. "If she's still somewhere in the Candy Kingdom, I promise we'll do anything we can to help you bring her back."

"You'd do that for us?" Funny bounced up and down. "You two really are heroes! Wait until Princess Cupcake hears about this!" Funny's dough coiled and uncoiled like a spring, and her stringy mouth stretched into a broad smile. "I knew there was a reason you have the same names as Gummo Bear royalty."

"You know Princess Cupcake personally?" Zeb's eyes lit up again with the Princess Interest. Only the word *trophy* made Zeb's eyes twinkle more. "Does she give out trophies, by chance?"

There he went again. Ellie sighed. "You're hopeless."

Funny's dad laughed. "It's rumored that Princess Cupcake has an early bedtime. You'll have to wait at least until morning to find out."

Bedtime! Oh, dear. The sun had faded almost completely, and soon the night would be pitch black. Ellie's stomach clenched. She and Zeb had nowhere to sleep in the Candy Kingdom, for one thing. But far worse, Grandma had to be home by now—and having a panic attack. Finding her grandchildren missing could put her in a worse state than hearing her cat had been hit by a car.

Possibly.

"Hey, Zeb," Ellie said, waving a hand in front of his glimmering, dazed eyes. "We can't stay until morning. We have to go."

"But Princess Cupcake!"

"Grandma will freak out if we're not there. Plus, if Mr. Grumpy Pants was actually hurt today . . ." It would make a terrible day for her even worse.

Princess Interest left Zeb's eyes. "Fine. I'm telling you, though, I have a theory that it's not really as late at home as you think."

"It's nighttime. We've been here for hours! Picture the anguish on Grandma's face." Surely, he could sympathize. "Worse, we didn't do what we said we'd do. We didn't clean the room. All we did was disobey her, and now, we might terrify her." Or break her heart, if they couldn't get home. "Please, Zeb? I trusted you before. Can you trust me now?"

Zeb's shoulders fell, but he didn't say anything.

"Mr. Funnel? Do you know if there's anything at the castle that lets people like . . . us"—she waved a pointer finger between herself and Zeb—"um, you know . . . travel?" How could she explain it without being too weird? "We come from somewhere else. Not Candy Kingdom."

"I have heard such rumors." Funny's dad looked as thoughtful as a pile of dough strings could look. "Nothing confirmed. I will accompany you if you like. I've never been to the castle myself, of course . . ."

Oh, dear. But they needed to hurry down the path to the castle. "We *need* to go home, Zeb."

"Look—it's only been about an hour." He flashed her the watch, and sure enough, it showed only an hour had gone by. "I'm sure we have time to see Princess Cupcake."

"Is that watch even ticking?" Ellie *knew* they'd been here longer.

The butterscotch candy sun had set. "It isn't . . . broken, is it?" That would be terrible. Ellie shouldn't have said it aloud.

Zeb looked stricken. "It's ticking. And I told you, I'd never forget to wind it. But just to reassure you, here." Zeb tugged at the pin and twisted it to tighten the internal spring. "I wound it this morning just like I do every—"

Morning. Ellie's mind filled in the blank, but she couldn't speak it. The world had gone black.

Love More Than Roses

Something sharp stabbed the center of Ellie's back. With rickety muscles, she sat up. "Ouch." From beneath her, she pulled a pointy little plastic Gummo Bear. "That thing's sharper than rose-trimming shears."

"Aw, dang it." Zeb lay face down on the carpet. "I think there's a tuft of Mr. Grumpy Pants's fur in my mouth." He dug it out and wiped it on his pant leg. "And you made it so I didn't get to meet the princess or get a trophy. Dang it, Ellie."

"I made it so?" Ellie rubbed the side of her head. "Hardly! I told you we needed to hurry down the path to the castle. That's where the princess lives, isn't it?"

"Not that. You forced me to wind the watch."

Oh. Yeah. It was the only thing that made sense. The second he wound the watch, they reappeared in Mr. Grumpy Pants's banana-smelling room.

Ellie looked around at the faded, yellow walls. Compared to the bright, candy-colored world they'd just left, this place felt even dimmer than it had before.

"See?" Zeb pointed to the clock on the far wall above the box of dried-apple-head dolls. "That clock matches the time on Grandpa's pocket watch. I told you we'd only been gone a few minutes." He put his chin on his hand and his elbow on his knee, disappointment incarnate.

"Sorry." She got up onto her knees and looked at the scattered playing pieces. "If it makes you feel better, I wanted to see Princess Cupcake, too."

Zeb didn't look like it made him feel better. "Now, we probably never will."

A door slammed in the front room.

"Grandma! Is that you?" She was home! Oh, thank goodness. Ellie scrambled to put away the game pieces and hissed, "At least we made it in time to keep Grandma from worrying." That was a lot more important than meeting a princess, no matter what Zeb moaned. "Besides, we saved the funnel cakes. They have their bridge back and their food for their babies. You were a hero, Zeb, trophy, or no trophy. Princess or no princess."

"Hero, huh?" For a moment, he brightened, but he soon plopped into dejection again. "If only there'd been a trophy. Maybe one encrusted with candy gems, or with a big, golden cup of chocolate. Gordo McTwigg's trophy collection would have been so jealous."

"Kids? Where are you?" Grandma Gretchen peeked her head in the door. "Oh, you're in Mr. Grumpy Pants's room, are you?" Her gaze fell on the game box. "I thought I asked you not to play with that game."

"You did, Grandma. We're sorry." A string of shame plucked

inside Ellie. She hadn't meant to purposely hurt Grandma.

Zeb looked up with guilt in his eyes.

Grandma Gretchen frowned for a second and then broke into a grin. "I guess I'm too happy about Mr. Grumpy Pants to be upset about anything else."

"Is there good news?"

"Yes, very good news. Mr. Grumpy Pants lives again. One life down, eight to go. The car hit him, but he revived."

Ellie exhaled. "Thank goodness!"

"That's incredible!" Zeb jumped up. "I want to show you something, Grandma." He jogged out of the room and was back in a few seconds. He had a book with flowers on the front. "See? This gardening book says the roses will come back, too. Just like Mr. G."

Grandma put an arm around him. "I knew they'd come back. It will just take a few weeks, and I had wanted to enjoy them for the summer. Your grandpa planted them for me."

"Oh." Zeb looked at the floor. "I'm sorry I ruined them for now."

"Well, I love you more than I love my roses, so let's leave it at that." She pulled her stiff, sorry grandson into an embrace. However, after a few seconds, he lifted his arms, and they relaxed into a mutual hug.

"And you love Mr. Grumpy Pants, too, right?" Ellie came over to join the hug. "Tell us what happened."

"Why don't I tell you over ice cream? We can celebrate. I picked up some vanilla."

"Ice cream!" Ellie and Zeb both gasped in unison, pulling out of the jumble of love. "But—"

"I know. It's probably not as good as raisin cookies, but because

I had to spend so long at the veterinarian's office, I didn't have time to bake."

"That's okay, Grandma. We're just glad the cat is well." Even if the cat hated her, Ellie was glad Mr. Grumpy Pants had survived the accident.

At that moment, in walked the cat. "Oh, hey, Mr. G." Zeb stooped down and picked him up. He still glared at Ellie. In a show of friendship, she reached out to pet him, but he extended a paw with his claws out. Ellie pulled her hand away just in time and shoved it in her pocket, where she only found some cookie crumbs.

The tinfoil and the dime and things are gone. I didn't imagine it all.

The four of them headed down the hallway to the kitchen, where Grandma Gretchen opened her freezer and pulled out a quart of ice cream. Sugar-free ice cream, sweetened with stevia, but who could complain?

"Do you want chocolate syrup on yours? I made some with carob root." Grandma bustled around in the kitchen, pulling out spoons and glass dishes.

Ellie blinked, keeping her eyes shut a little longer than usual. Painted on the inside of her eyelids, she saw the Candy Kingdom spread out in all its colorful glory. *What was the next place on the game board after Lake Cocoa*? Ellie should have looked. There was so much more they hadn't seen before the watch-winding yanked them back to reality.

However, no way would Ellie endanger Grandma's trust in them again—nor would she jeopardize Grandma's peace of mind. Their return had been far too close of a close call.

No, the rest of their stay at Grandma Gretchen's would be—what? Relaxing?

Besides, being happy together and seeing Grandma's smile was better than the game—even if Grandma was putting sliced old bananas and raisin cookie crumbles on top of all their scooped ice cream.

Now that Funny's family could access Lake Cocoa, maybe they wouldn't have any reason to go back to the Candy Kingdom. *Except that I promised to help find Funny's sister because Mr. Funnel Cake believes his girl is still out there somewhere. And Zeb hasn't seen the princess or received his trophy.*

No. Ellie couldn't think that way. Being with Grandma Gretchen and Mr. Grumpy Pants was enough. Maybe they could weed the garden and clean the cat's bedroom and put together some puzzles. That would be fun. After all, they only had a few days left here. A short time.

Zeb would know exactly how long, right down to the hour and the minute.

Ellie glanced at Grandpa's watch. How had it brought them home? She'd never dreamed it was a magical watch, connecting Grandma's house with a board game. But of course! It only made sense that something of Grandpa's would be linked with Grandma's house, and with her love!

Indeed, Zeb wasn't the only one who could come up with theories.

"After we finish our ice cream, do you want to put together the winter scene puzzle with me, Grandma?" Ellie settled in a chair at the table. "Or maybe we could scrub the walls together."

"That would be so nice. Now, about the adventure with the cat." Grandma sat down beside them, placing a bowl of ice cream in front of each of them. "It all started when Mr. Nabor was backing out of the driveway . . ."

Grandma told the whole, harrowing story, and she exhaled at the end. "But all's well that ends well."

"That's right." Ellie scooped the last drop of sweet vanilla cream from her dish.

"By the way, kids. Have either of you seen my gardening shears?"

Ellie looked at Zeb. Zeb looked at Ellie.

We left them in the Candy Kingdom!

Candy Kingdom The Desserted Island

Coming Soon...

"So, you're saying the funnel cake people's lives are better, but the Taffy Colony is having more trouble?" Ellie asked.

And it was Zeb and Ellie's fault.

"If you call being rounded up like cattle and threatened within an inch of our elasticity, yes." Daffy the Taffy turned around and continued hopping down the pathway, over the bridge and into full view of Lake Cocoa—the middle of which contained a tower.

"The princess's tower," Zeb breathed.

"Exactly." Daffy hopped with more vigor. "And to think! Jinja is trying to use my family as the springs for his catapults to destroy her fortress!" Daffy's voice quavered. "Our own princess, and we're being used as weapons against her."

Ellie grabbed Zeb's hand, gripping it hard. Without her saying a word, he knew exactly what she wanted to communicate to him: that they had to help the Taffy Colony.

AUTHOR

Jenny Griffith worked in a cookie factory. She loves board games, candy, and grandparents. She's not great at jigsaw puzzles, but her daughters are. Her five kids keep bringing home the world's grumpiest cats. Jenny's favorite candies seem to always be the ones everyone else thinks are nasty.

ILLUSTRATOR

Elysse is a passionate artist with a sweet tooth for baked goods and nut-filled chocolate, and a love for sour gummy candies! While growing up, she enjoyed the delicious aroma and taste of her mother's old-fashioned homemade caramels and other sweet treats filling her home. And a visit to grandma's house was never complete without sneaking a cookie (or three) from her jar on the counter. She's happily married to her sweetheart, and they love playing board games together.

CPSIA information can be obtained
at www.ICGtesting.com
Printed in the USA
LVHW072345300321
682970LV00018B/2077